Loo Queue

Nicholas Allan

RED FOX

Pink Elephant is here,
the first to go to the loo.

1 **One** animal queues
to do what he must do.

Yellow Rhino is next
to join the end of the queue.

THE LOO

2 **Two** animals queue
to do what they must do.

Green Giraffe arrives
with a **skip**, a **jump** and a . . .

3 **Three** animals queue to do what they must do.

Blue Bear, he looks so sad.
"Boo hoo hoo!"

THE LOO

4 **Four** animals queue to do what they must do.

Orange Tiger comes along
to cheer up poor old Blue.

5 **Five** animals queue
to do what they must do.

Bouncy, bouncy, bouncy **bounce**
comes **Purple Kangaroo**.

6 But **six** animals are tired of waiting in a queue!

So they all shout together:

"Hurry up, you!"

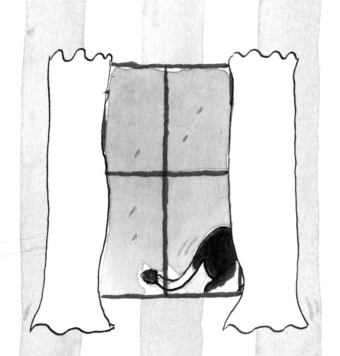

But no one comes out.

"Let's take a peekaboo."
They open the door and find . . .

No one in the loo!

Oh, how the animals argue -
what a hullabaloo!

Then . . .

SLAM!

Now there's someone in there,
someone new – but **who**?

Here's a **COW** all black and white.
Who moos, and moos, and **moos!**

 **Seven** animals queue to do what they must do.

Flying down to join them
is **Indigo Cockatoo**.

8 **Eight** animals queue to do what they must do.

Turquoise Hippo looks so cute in his ballet tutu.

9 **Nine** animals queue to do what they must do.

And finally comes along a tiny **Crimson Shrew.**

10 **Ten** animals queue
to do what they must do.

So they all shout together:

"Hurry up, you!"

The door slowly opens.
Something comes in view.
And a deep, **deep** voice says . . .

Now no one needs the loo!

And so, **at last**, it's free for . . .

YOU!
(To do just what you need to do.)